Taken

Written by Baylee Carlyon

©2024 Baylee Carlyon

Written by Baylee Carlyon

Cover Design illustrated by Baylee Carlyon

ISBN: 978-1-7637018-0-9

Dedication

To Melissa my amazing mentor, Barry my encouraging Dad, and Robin my supportive enthusiastic cousin.

Table of Contents

CHAPTER 1: My life.

Gary and Lilly were walking home from school and passed their friend, Timmy's, house.

'Did you hear Timmy disappeared last night?' Lilly said.

'Not another one!' said Gary, 'Isn't that the third kid in the last month?'

'Maybe, though I think this is the fourth,' Lilly replied. Gary rolled his eyes. His sister was always annoyingly correcting him.

Gary walked ahead of Lilly.

'That will never happen to us,' he said. 'We wouldn't be so stupid to get taken. I don't want to talk about this, let's change the subject. Didn't dad say he would have a surprise for us when he got home?'

'Maybe we're going to move back to the farm?' Lilly said hopefully. 'I miss my pony.'

'It wasn't your pony, silly,' said Gary, 'It belonged to Farmer Jones, and he just let you ride it occasionally.'

Lilly poked her tongue out at Gary.

'Don't be so picky,' Lilly said. 'I still miss that pony. I wish dad hadn't lost his job when Farmer Jones passed away.'

'Yeah, me too,' Gary said. 'We better hurry up, dad will be home soon, and we can find out what the surprise is. Race you!' Gary started running.

'Wait for me,' Lilly complained running to catch up with her twin brother. They arrived on their front porch out of breath and laughing.

'There you both are,' their mum greeted at the door. 'Why are you so late, I was starting to worry you had been taken too.'

'We weren't that late,' said Gary.

'Go inside, get out of your uniform. You can have your snack on the porch and wait for your dad there,' said mum with an annoyed tone in her voice.

Gary and Lilly ran upstairs, knowing to do as they were told when their mum was annoyed. As they went past the front room, they heard their grandma talk to their mum.

'It's okay, Amy, they're home now, safe and sound,' Grandma said.

After they had changed clothes and eaten their snack, Gary and Lilly were playing soccer in the front yard, waiting for their dad to come home from work.

They heard their dad's van coming up their street long before they saw it. He pulled into the driveway, his van coughing out smoke. As he put it in park, the smoking stopped. He jumped out of the van.

'Hey kids,' he said.

Gary and Lilly abandoned their soccer game and ran to their dad.

'Where's our surprise?' Lilly asked.

'Hang on, give me a minute," said their dad. He waved to his wife and his mum and turned to the back of his van and opened the door. He rummaged through the mess and found what he was looking for and he passed Gary a cardboard box. Lilly snatched the box from him, put it on the ground and opened the lid.

'A puppy!' she gasped, then giggled as a little black puppy tried to scramble out of the box.

Gary pushed his sister aside to see the puppy himself.

'I picked this little guy up from your Uncle Bob's house, Maisie had puppies, and he thought you would like one,' their dad said.

They lifted the puppy out of the box and started to play with it on the porch. Their parents went inside, discussing the disappearing children.

'Come on kids, bring the puppy inside,' their mum called to them. 'You know you're not supposed to play outside by yourselves.'

Gary and Lilly groaned, but they picked up the puppy and dragged themselves into the loungeroom and sat on the floor and fought over who would hold the puppy. Lilly won and the puppy sat on Lilly's lap. The puppy tried to catch her finger as she dangled it back and forth in front of her face.

'What do you think we should call her?' he asked his sister.

Lilly thought for a moment before replying, 'Coco.'

'That's a boring name,' replied Gary, 'What about Midnight, that's a good, strong name for a dog.'

'Nah,' said Lilly, 'That sounds like a name for a bushranger. She's too cute for that. Her name is Coco.' Lilly said it in a tone that Gary knew better than to argue with.

He rolled his eyes and got up to go to his bedroom to find a toy for the puppy.

He was rummaging through his old toy box to find a teddy when he heard strange noises coming from downstairs and went to investigate.

CHAPTER 2: The men in blue boiler suits

Gary reached the top of the stairs just in time to see two strange men in the lounge room. They were both dressed in dark blue boiler suits that were obviously old and quite dirty. There was a yellow badge on the breast pocket of each suit. One man was blocking the door to the kitchen, and the other was trying to grab Lilly. Coco was running around, barking, and trying to trip up the men. He could hear his parents banging on the kitchen door, trying to get to the lounge room. Lilly was trying to run to the stairs to get away.

'Lilly!!' Gary shouted, running down the stairs so fast he tripped over his shoelaces and landed face first on the landing.

Seeing Gary, the men looked at each other and called out to their parents, 'You got another one! Don't mind if we take this kid too?'

They heard their parents' muffled screams and banging on the door.

The men shrugged their shoulders.

'I take that as a yes,' one of them said sarcastically.

Gary scrambled to stand up and head back to his bedroom but heard Lilly scream for help. He ran to help her, and they headed for the front door to escape.

They opened the front door only to find a third man standing there. Lilly and Gary were trapped, and the men grabbed hold of them. Even though they tried to fight back, the men were too big, and they were outnumbered. Coco tried to bite them on their ankles, but one of the men kicked her away and she cowered under the sofa.

The men carried Gary and Lilly out the front door and pushed the kids in the back of their van. As the door of the van closed, the siblings heard their parents barging through the front door, screaming their names. The men got in the front of the van, started the engine and quickly zoomed away.

The van bumped along the road and Gary and Lilly clung to each other in fear. Gary tried to pay attention to where they were going, but the van had no windows in the back. Soon the movement of the van lulled them to sleep.

CHAPTER 3: Gary

Gary woke up. He was lying on a wooden floor, and it took him a little while to register that he wasn't at home in his living room.

He stretched and looked around the small room. It was empty with wooden walls and a dirty window that barely let in any light. He saw a boy who looked a bit younger than him with sandy blonde hair and freckles on his nose standing near a door. Before Gary could say anything, the boy started to speak.

'At last, you've woken up, I'm Justin this is for you,' he said holding out a broom. Gary got to feet, still in a daze, and followed the boy out of the room and into a large shed.

'Where am I?' asked Gary.

Just then a big hand smacked them both over the back of the head.

'Get a move on. More sweep, less chit chat boys.' Gary saw the hand belonged to a big, fat man who reminded him of a bowling ball. He was wearing the same blue boiler suit as the men who had taken them. Gary stared as the man strode down the other end of the shed.

Gary looked around and saw the shed was huge. Cracked lights and rotten wood balconies hung over his head. He could see a number of boys around his age, all doing various jobs. Some boys were standing at long tables sorting something. Others were carting large, heavy buckets from the tables to one end of the shed. There were no girls anywhere to be seen, however there were a few men wearing the same blue boiler suits as the men who had snatched Gary and Lilly walking between the tables and standing on the balcony.

Justin started to explain what they needed to do. Gary didn't hear half of what he said because he was looking around thinking… *I'm in a terrible place, I need to get out of here but how?* Then he realised there was no sign of Lilly.

'Where are we?' Gary asked Justin again. 'What's going on? Where is my sister?'

'Shhh, not now,' Justin said. 'We need to do this work, or we'll get in trouble. Talk later.'

Gary picked up the broom and began sweeping, all the time he was looking around to see how he could find his sister, though he did think he saw his friend Timmy at the other end of the shed.

He froze as he saw a mean looking man walked in his direction. The man stopped a few metres away, then turned around and yelled at Timmy who was apparently sweeping in the wrong spot. Gary took the opportunity to rummage through his pockets careful not to make a single sound as he searched certain he would find something that could help him find Lilly and then escape together.

As Gary was busy looking in his pockets, he hadn't noticed two workers walk up in front of him. He was just about to start sweeping again, when one of the men grabbed him.

'You're coming with us to dig up gold and crystals,' the man snarled.

As he marched Gary out of the shed, he shot dirty looks at kids who had stopped to watch the action. He held Gary tightly as he struggled to get out of the man's grip. He wanted to find Lilly. He hoped his sister was safe somewhere, maybe working as a slave as well and he was going to find her no matter what.

The man marched Gary outside towards a river where there were other boys also working. He was instructed to pick up dirty crystals and gold nuggets that were lying on the ground and sort them into large buckets.

As he toiled, he daydreamed about reuniting with Lilly. Gary hadn't noticed he was slowing until a man placed five more empty buckets in front of him and kicked him roughly to wake him up from his daydream.

'Hurry up, we have a quota to fill,' the man barked at him before moving on. Gary did as he was told, all the while seeing if there was an opportunity to escape. He was also worried about Lilly, hoping she was okay.

It wasn't too much longer before the man returned and grabbed the full buckets before announcing, 'We are going back to the camp; the boss has news.'

Gary lined up with the other kids, ready to walk back to the camp. He studied their dirty faces and thought, some are not even eight years old yet. Gary wanted to yell and scream and say something, but he guessed it will be safer to keep his mouth shut, at least for now.

As they walked, Gary hummed quietly to himself. The other kids were staring at him, but he didn't care, he only wanted to find his sister.

When they arrived back at the camp, they were instructed to stand in age group lines. Gary noticed that the boys were on one side of the yard, and the girls were on the other. They were surrounded by mean looking guards.

Gary was relieved to spot Lilly on the other side of the yard lined up with the girls and happy to see that she looked unharmed. Their eyes met and Lilly's face lit up in recognition.

Before Gary could think any more, the boss got up and stood on the stage in front of them.

'We're moving camp. All of you will be coming with us. The buses are waiting.'

The guards started to herd the children towards the gates and chaos reigned. The boys and girls got mixed in together and Gary and Lilly moved towards each other.

'Thank goodness you're okay, Gary, I was so worried.' Lilly said when they caught up with each other.

'I'm glad you're okay too,' said Gary. They gave each other a hug, which is something they would never usually do, before being carried along with the crowd towards the buses.

As they were nearing the last bus, Gary spotted a dumpster and noticed the guards were distracted. He grabbed Lilly's hand, and they slipped away with the dumpster hiding them from the men's view.

They ducked down and could get a feel for what was happening from under the dumpster. They held their breath as they saw the feet of a guard go past.

'That's everyone, boss,' the guard called. 'Let's go.'

Gary and Lilly waited until the last bus was out of sight. When they were sure there were no guards left, they started running towards a massive hill in the distance, in the opposite direction from the buses.

They ran for what felt like an eternity, the sun started going down and Gary and Lilly were exhausted.

'Gary! Psst over here.' Lilly whispered loudly from a dark place behind him. He turned around to see his sister in a cave. He ran toward her as fast as he could and tumbled into the cave after her.

The floor of the cave was rocky, but smooth enough for them to sit on to have a bit of rest.

Gary and Lilly settled in for the night and decided to work out how they would get home tomorrow.

CHAPTER 4: A plan to get home.

The next morning, Gary stretched and noticed that Lilly was already awake and had been drawing symbols in the sand on the floor of the cave.

'What are you doing?' asked Gary.

'Making a plan, dummy,' said Lilly in a tone that indicated it should be obvious.

'A plan for what?'

'To get home,' said Lilly.

'But we don't know where we are,' said Gary.

'That's what this is all about,' she said, indicating her symbols. 'I have a plan.'

Gary stared at his sister as she started explaining what she had come up with. It really didn't make sense to Gary, and it wasn't long before his mind started to wander.

'Gary, are you listening? Or do I have to go over the plan again,' Lilly teased. Gary had been wondering if the kids from the camp were safe and had not heard his sister talking to him.

'Earth to Gary,' she said, clicking her fingers in front of his face.

'I was just thinking about the other kids in the camp,' Gary said. 'Should we go back and try to help them?'

'Don't think about it, we have to follow the plan,' she said. 'When we get home, we can alert the police to let them know about the other kids.'

'Are you sure?' asked Gary.

'We're just kids ourselves,' said Lilly, 'How can we help them? Besides, we don't know where they've gone, and we can't keep up with buses.'

Gary could see her point and reluctantly agreed. He asked Lilly to repeat the plan again, which made Lilly growl, but she repeated it.

When Lilly was sure Gary understood the plan, they decided to get started. Lilly motioned for Gary to follow her silently outside the cave. While they were quite sure the bad guys hadn't noticed they had escaped, they still wanted to be careful.

The siblings made their way through the forest and felt like they had been walking for hours, searching for food and their way home when they saw some drops of blood. They followed a blood trail and soon a bad smell helped them find a wild pig with a broken spear in its stomach. Hunters must have speared the animal, and it had been able to get away before it died.

Gary went over to the pig and pulled the spear out to inspect it.

'Cool point on this, it looks like someone carved it with bare hands,' he said. Lilly looked at him with disgust.

'Ewww, that's gross Gary,' she said and walked away.

He wiped the spear on the grass and followed his sister, taking the broken spear with him.

They could hear a waterfall not too far away and started toward it as they were both very thirsty. They came out of the bush onto a rocky crystal-clear creek, so they stopped and drank the cold water until they were full.

Gary could see schools of small fish and a few bigger ones and decided to try to spear them, as he had seen people do on TV shows. He tried for a long time to spear them from the bank with no luck.

'You get in and chase them towards me and I will try and spear them,' he said, and Lilly was so hot in the midday sun she happily got into the water.

After twenty minutes, it was still not helping so Gary jumped in too and splashed about with Lilly forgetting how hungry he was.

When they were getting tired, the siblings sat on some big warm rocks to dry off.

'Gary if we can't catch any fish; can't we eat berries instead,' Lilly sighed as she started to climb off the tall rocks they were on and heading to some bushes growing beside the pool with red coloured fruit.

Gary followed her putting the broken spear in his pocket as he walked down to join her, his sister was picking berries off a bush.

Gary started to help her pick them.

'This is way better than fish,' she mumbled her mouth full of berries.

Gary wasn't sure they should be eating these as they could be poisonous, but Lilly seemed to be enjoying them and not feeling sick, so he put a berry in his mouth and nodded. Berry juice stained their T-shirts as they stuffed their mouths with a couple more handfuls, then saving the rest for later.

Gary began wandering further into the bushes followed by Lilly who was still stuffing her mouth with berries. Gary twirled around and took them off her before she ate them all.

'Hey, I was eating them,' she laughed.

'You're slowing us down eating all the time,' he said bossily.

'Fine, I'll stop eating,' she said rubbing her hand. 'We probably should get moving to get home.'

Before they could get going again, Gary froze as he heard angry voices echoing through the trees.

'Shhh,' he said to Lilly, 'Do you hear that?'

'Hear what?' she said.

'I think the bad guys are nearby, we'd better get moving.'

The siblings nodded and started moving as quietly as they could away from the voices.

CHAPTER 5: Bakery.

Gary and Lilly moved until they could no longer hear the voices and then they realised they could smell the delicious scent of freshly baked bread in the air.

'I think there's a bakery,' said Lilly.

'You're right,' said Gary. 'Maybe they can help us?'

'Let's go and see,' said Lilly.

They carefully made their way through the trees until they saw the back of a building and crept inside.

'Hello,' The siblings jumped as a man greeted them. 'What are you doing here?'

Gary thought quickly.

'We're lost, do you think you can help us get home?'

'I'm sure we can,' the man said, 'Come through and meet my wife. Are you both hungry?'

Gary and Lilly nodded and followed the man through into a sitting room and told to wait. They didn't have to wait long before a woman came in carrying a tray with juice and croissants. She put them down on a coffee table and invited them to help themselves.

'My husband says you're lost. You're both safe now, I'm sure we can help you get home,' the woman said to them.

Gary and Lilly shoved the food into their mouths, eating hungrily.

'You both look exhausted,' the woman said. 'Why don't you stay for dinner and sleep, and we'll see what we can do to get you home in the morning.'

The siblings thanked the woman. Lilly helped the woman to make dinner, and they all sat down to eat.

As they were eating, Gary spotted a photo on the dining room wall that looked familiar.

'Who's that?' he asked, pointing at the photo.

'That's our son,' the man replied. 'Justin. He's been missing for a few months.'

Gary and Lilly exchanged a glance and wondered if they should tell the couple that Gary had seen Justin in the camp. Something about the tone of the man's voice made Gary keep quiet, along with the fact that something wasn't right about the photo. He had a closer look and saw the kid in the picture had six fingers on one hand.

Instead, he yawned noisily and said he was sleepy and ready for bed.

The woman gestured for the kids to follow her into another room with two soft beds. They said goodnight and, even though Gary and Lilly felt something wasn't quite right, they were exhausted and soon fell into a dreamless sleep.

Gary woke up in the middle of the night, he thought he heard some familiar voices. He quietly got out of bed and crept to the door to eavesdrop. He listened for a few minutes, then went to Lilly's bed and shook her awake. He put his hand over her mouth as she let out a muffled scream.

'Shhh, I don't think we're safe here. Let's skedaddle,' he whispered.

Lilly looked confused and annoyed. She flung the blanket over her head and tried to go back to sleep. Gary shook her again and told her to listen. They could hear the voices of the men who had captured them talking about hanging around to take the kids back to camp in the morning.

'OK,' Lilly whispered, 'Let's go.'

Both kids trembled with fear as they quietly opened the window and slipped outside. They made their way to the bushes on the edge of town and found somewhere to hide in some thick bushes as the sun started to rise.

Lilly pointed down to her hand and Gary saw a large cut. He found some banana leaves to wrap around it to stop the bleeding.

Lilly curled up and started to cry with pain and fear. Gary gave her a hug and told her: "We will make it home I promise you. We need to be quiet until we can run from here.'

Just then, they heard voices.

CHAPTER 6: Running in the bush.

As the voices were getting closer, Gary recognised them as the man from the camp, the baker and his wife.

'They're looking for us,' Lilly whispered softly, shaking her head in disbelief.

'We need to get out of here,' Gary whispered back.

He started to look at the trees in the distance. When he turned, he saw the men burst out into the open and Gary ducked down behind some bushes, dragging Lilly down with him. One of the men stood there, seconds later the baker joined him.

'I thought I heard them over here,' the baker said. He stood so close to where Lilly and Gary were hiding that they could smell the stale cigarette smoke on his clothes.

Gary and Lilly held their breath, too scared to move. Then Gary looked down to see lots of little pebbles at his feet and began throwing them in the opposite direction.

'What was that?' one guy asked as he looked in the direction he had thrown the pebbles. Gary gulped as the men strode past.

'That was close,' Gary whispered when the grown-ups were out of sight. "We need to get out of here."

Lilly began heading towards the nearest trees, followed by Gary. They walked quickly on, stopping occasionally to make sure they hadn't been followed.

After a while, Lilly started lagging behind.

'Lilly, hurry up,' he said turning to his sister who was picking bananas. He ran towards his sister.

'Gary, stop worrying,' Lilly said passing him a banana when he reached her. 'We've left the bad people behind; we can take a moment to eat something.' He took it and started to peel it quickly.

'Hurry up,' Lilly teased and started walking ahead of him.

'Ha-ha very funny,' he said running to join her then nearly banging into her as she stopped to stare at something.

'It's the camp,' Gary gasped when he recognized it. The place had been burnt to the ground! They trotted towards it, coughing as the smell of the burnt building filled the air around them.

'Gary, what happened?' Lilly asked. He was too busy staring at the smouldering ashes to reply. 'Does this mean we've been walking around in circles this whole time?'

'I guess so,' said Gary, feeling disappointed.

Gary walked on so he could have a closer look at the burnt wood of the building.

'Gary let's go,' Lilly said stepping backwards. Just then a big spider crawled out of the embers, and Lilly screamed in terror, 'I hate spiders!'

Gary ran up quickly to join her, noticing the spider was a venomous red-back.

'Maybe we should have a bit of a look around first?' said Gary, 'We might get a clue to where we are.'

'Fine, you look around,' Lilly said, 'I need a rest, I'm going to sit and wait here.' Lilly sat cross-legged on the ground and nursed her aching hand.

Gary walked off and inspected the remains of the camp. He found a burned map that didn't tell him anything, along with some other burned documents. He started feeling very discouraged.

'Okay, I'm done,' he said joining Lilly. 'Let's get out of here.'

'Gary, which way?' Lilly asked. He looked around to see three pathways between the trees. One they had followed before, one the bad guys took the other kids, and one they hadn't explored before.

'Umm this one,' he said pointing at the far left one before trotting towards it. Lilly followed close behind him, it looked darker once they went past the first few bushes and trees. The siblings wandered in that direction

hoping they would avoid any sign of the bad
men.

CHAPTER 7: A not so perfect adventure.

The two of them walked briskly through the trees. Gary noticed that Lilly was starting to slow down.

'Come on, Grandma!' he said as he turned and ran past her. 'Beat you!' She laughed and ran after him.

'There's my brother,' she joked, as she stopped to catch her breath.

'Woohoo!! I win,' Gary cheered, high fiving his sister. She had a smile on her face.

'You only won because you started first,' she teased, skipping away from him... 'and didn't tell me where the finish line was.'

He danced happily and punched the air before following her.

As they walked further into the bush, a loud snort filled the air. Lilly followed the sound, and it led to a horse which was trying to pull its halter rope free from a tree where it had become wedged.

Lilly stepped forward and strode towards the trapped animal. Gary stopped her just as the horse turned to stare at them.

'You can't walk up on a creature you don't know,' he said, as he turned to pick some apples off a nearby tree to offer the horse. Lilly, having ridden horses since she was six, crossed her arms grumbling even though she knew he was right.

'Oh, stop complaining Lilly,' Gary said walking back to her and sharing the apples.

'Here you go have an apple,' Gary said quietly to the horse. Lilly petted the horse's nose, and it licked her hand like a dog.

Gary reached up and untangled the horse's halter rope from the tree. They walked with the horse through the bush, following the horse's lead as it seemed to know where it was going.

 A couple of minutes later they arrived at an old shed in the middle of a paddock, that had clearly been used to keep horses as it had a trough outside, although the fences had been knocked down.

'We can stay here for the night!' Gary said. The shed looked cosy and warm, with space for the siblings as well as the horse.

'Gary what are you doing?' Lilly asked a little while later. Gary was trying to get a fire to start with two sticks.

'We have to stay warm,' he said, then suddenly thunder rumbled through the sky followed by large drops of rain. The siblings ran into the shed to shelter for the rest of the night, thoughts of a fire forgotten.

Gary and Lilly were hiding as lightning flicked across the grey sky, thunder rumbled loudly once again, and rain splashed down outside. The horse reared up and Lilly jumped up to calm it down.

'Whoa girl, it's okay, a little noise can't hurt us,' she said softly. Gary rolled his eyes.

Just then, Gary and Lilly looked out the window and saw a lightning strike hit a nearby tree, causing it to burst into flames and fall on top of the shed. The siblings were able to escape, just before the shed got squished like a banana. The horse galloped away in fear, too fast for Gary and Lilly to catch him.

It didn't take long for the bush around the shed to burst into flames around them as the two kids ran to find safety.

'A little noise can't hurt us?!' Gary shouted sarcastically as they ran.

'That was not 'a little' noise! There,' Lilly shouted before pointing at a cave entrance she could see in the light of the flames. They made their way to the cave. It was sitting on a rock ledge, so they climbed up and tumbled in.

Gary took a moment to look out at where they had come. Lightning and thunder still flicked across the sky, and now it was joined by a large black cloud from the bush fire that was growing quickly.

Gary grabbed Lilly's arm.

'We should get further into the cave and let the fire pass,' he said, dragging her further into the cave.

They moved and found a place they could lie down to let the fire burn out, and then make their way out in the morning.

They tried to fall asleep as the noises of the storm and the fire kept them awake. They were eventually able to get some fitful sleep.

CHAPTER 8: The city and the horse.

The next morning, Gary and Lilly were happy to see that the cave wasn't pitch black, so they decided to see if they could walk through the cave instead of going back the way they came.

They walked for what felt like ages before coming out at the other side of the mountain.

Looking out, they saw a large grass paddock surrounded by a lot of trees, including some fruit trees. In the distance, they could see a city, so figured they must be on the right track.

Gary and Lilly made their way down the side of the mountain where they picked some fruit to eat and filled their pockets so they would have some for later.

'Hey, look at that,' Lilly said. 'Isn't that the horse we rescued?'

Gary looked up to see a horse in the middle of the paddock eating grass.

'Maybe we can catch it and ride it for a while?' Lilly said. 'My feet are sore from walking.'

Gary agreed and they went slowly toward the horse. Lilly caught hold of the halter rope that was still around its neck and she spoke to it softly.

'Woo Hoo!' Gary cheered, startling the horse. Lilly gave him an evil look.

'Gary!' she exclaimed. 'Why did you do that?'

'Sorry,' Gary mumbled.

Lilly held onto the rope and tried to calm it down. The horse tugged at the rope and Lilly tried not to cry out as it made her sore hand hurt even more.

Gary noticed his sister struggling and took the rope out of her hand and helped her calm the horse.

When the horse was calm, Lilly led it close to a large rock and climbed on.

'Come on Gary, up behind me,' she said, 'This will help us get home quicker.'

Gary tried to get on the horse, and slipped off, landing on his bottom before trying again. This time he was successful.

'Right,' Lilly said, 'Let's head towards the city, hopefully that gets us to home.'

CHAPTER 9: A Home in Sight.

The siblings rode the horse through the open fields, heading towards the city, until they arrived at the top of a cliff. When they got there, they could see the city more clearly and a beach at the bottom. They could see angry waves crashing against the rocks. They decided to stop for a break and climbed down off the horse.

'I wish a waterhole was nearby, I am so fricking thirsty,' Lilly complained as she sat down on a wet patch of grass.

'I'm sure there is something around here somewhere,' he said. He looked around and saw a small waterfall a bit further along the cliff. 'Look, there must a stream!'

Gary dragged Lilly to her feet and they led
the horse closer to the waterfall. The two of
them cheered when they saw there was a
stream. They secured the horse near the
water so she could have a drink too.

Lilly jumped in happily filling her hands with
water and drinking it at rapid speed.

'Lilly, save me some,' Gary laughed taking off
his T-shirt. Seconds later, he jumped into the
stream. As he splashed around, a fish swam
towards him. He quickly grabbed it then held
it tightly above the water as he climbed out.
The fish wriggled in his hand as he tried to
find a good time to spear it. Eventually he
speared the fish and washed his hands in the
stream. Lilly jumped out as the fish blood
drifted over towards her. She sat down on
the rocks as Gary came over to her and sat
down. He grabbed two nearby sticks and

began rubbing them together. A few minutes later he lit a small fire to cook the fish.

As they were eating, Lilly looked up and gasped, shaking Gary's shoulder, as she looked at the other side of the stream. In the bushes two men in blue boiler suits stood there watching them. Gary looked to see what his sister was looking at.

'Do you think they're with the bad men?' Lilly asked.

'Maybe,' Gary said, 'Just in case, we should go now.'

They quickly put out the fire, then climbed back onto the horse and galloped away as quickly as they could. The horse stopped at the edge of the forest and Lilly gasped. Just over the horizon was a city they recognized and their home.

They stared at their home for a couple of minutes before getting off the horse to lead her down a steep hill on their right.

Just then Lilly slipped, and booty scootered down the hill. Gary ran down to join her covering his mouth to muffle his giggles to hide them from her. As she got up wiping dirt off her clothes, she glared at him.

'Shut up!' she said angrily before stomping away. Gary followed her, still holding onto the horse's halter rope.

'That was so funny, you should have seen your face,' Gary said. Lilly poked her tongue at him.

'See ya, Gary,' Lilly laughed racing down the rest of the hill.

'Hey! Lilly! Wait up,' he said, running after her. A few minutes later they arrived at the entrance of a forest. Lilly walked in its direction, with Gary close behind her.

'Lilly come on this way,' he said, pointing at a canopy of trees. 'It'll be better for the horse.' Lilly turned to look at him. She pointed in the same direction to annoy him, and Gary rolled his eyes at her.

'Oops, sorry,' she said sarcastically as she shrugged her shoulders. The two of them walked into the bushy land. As they wandered into the trees Lilly looked at her shoes.

'Do you miss dad and mama?' she asked. Gary turned to look at her.

'Of course I do, but I know I will see them again soon,' he said, wrapping his arms around her as tears fell down her face.

'Okay Gary, promise me we stay together this whole trip,' she sobbed, wiping her nose on her sleeve. Gary smiled and pulled away from his sister's arms. He secured the horse then he sat down at the bottom of a tree. Lilly came and sat down next to him. As they talked, Gary tried to light a fire.

'Gary, we don't have anything to cook,' she said. Her brother pointed at a wild pig eating in the distance.

'Are you crazy? That pig will squish you!!' she gasped, grabbing her brother to stop him from running towards it as he got up.

'I'll be fine Lilly, don't worry,' he said gently taking his sister's hand away from his arm, then he bent down to grab the spear. Lilly held her breath, as Gary climbed the tree next to the pig and started aiming his spear. As he was about to throw it, the branch bent, dropping toward the ground, he made a noise, and the pig turned around and saw him. The pig tried to strike him with its tusks.

Gary tried to scramble further up the tree, but soon was hanging off the branch for dear life. Lilly screamed jumping up as the pig rubbed one tusk on the side of his leg, causing his knee to bleed.

'Get away from my brother!!' she shouted angrily. She climbed the tree, snatched the spear from Gary, and aimed it at the creature's back as it tried to strike Gary... this was not going to be easy.

The two of them might have to fight it together.

CHAPTER 10: The wrestle with the pig.

Lilly crouched on the branch and focused on the pig below her.

'Lilly, be careful!' Gary gasped as his sister got ready to stab the angry pig. She jumped on the pig's back and stabbed it, blood sprayed as the creature fell to the ground. Lilly stepped down as blood covered her whole body.

'Ewww, that was so gross!' she said in disgust.

'Lilly that was awesome!' he said clutching his hurt knee, it was still bleeding but it had calmed down. He walked towards the animal. 'Nice work sis, take that you fat pig.'

Lilly laughed before walking over to him to help move the massive pig to the fire.

'It's so heavy!' Gary complained dropping the pig. Lilly dropped her end and came over to him.

'I know but we need to eat, we might not find anything tomorrow,' she explained to him. Gary sighed and picked up the pig again. Lilly ran to the other end and started walking backwards towards the fire.

Eventually the siblings got the animal to their destination. Lilly sat down beside the tree.

'Whew, that took longer than I thought,' Gary said sitting down on the ground. He then managed to cut a leg from the pig and place it on the fire.

As the two of them ate the animal, a snake wriggled up behind Lilly. Gary spotted it at once and threw his spear toward it. Lilly didn't realise why he had done this a yelled, 'Gary, what the heck?' She jumped on him. As they wrestled, Lilly kicked Gary on the leg.

'Ooowww!!' he cried clutching his leg. 'Lilly, why did you do that?' and hopped away from his sister.

'Sorry bro, but it was an accident,' she snapped back walking away in the opposite direction just then the snake leaped at her.

'Aaaaggggggghhhhhh!!!' Lilly screamed, Jumping backwards towards Gary's side.

'Lilly what don't you understand when I say get lost sister!!' he screamed at her as she walked onto his side of the fire. She glared at him angrily as she stomped towards him.

'I'm sorry your majesty, do you mind being a little less stupid,' she said in a sarcastic voice.

'You did not say any of that.' Gary stared at his sister, 'I'm sorry Lilly,' he mumbled. Lilly gasped.

'For what?' she asked quietly. Gary looked away from her.

'For being a jerk to you,' he finished saying. Lilly jumped forwards wrapping her arms around him. He gasped before wrapping his arms around her.

'I'm sorry for being mean to you, too,' she said. They sat and ate their meal in silence, then tried to settle down to sleep for the night.

CHAPTER 11: The friendly wolf.

The next morning, they made sure the fire was out, and were disappointed to see the horse had wandered off. They hadn't gone long before they were happy to find a small water hole. They bent down for a drink. They scooped water in their hands and a wolf snuck up on them in silence.

'Wow,' Gary said, when he looked up to see the wolf. Lilly, who had been busy drinking, also glanced up to see what her brother was looking at.

'A-aa wolf,' she whispered. Her eyes were full of terror just as the wolf whimpered and its eyes softened. The kids then realised it was actually a young husky that was just as afraid of them. They slowly walked towards it and the dog lay down on its side just like pet dogs do when they want a pat.

'Aww what a cutie,' the two of them said rubbing the dog behind the ears. After a while spent stroking the animal, Gary stood up.

'Come on Lilly, let's go,' he said helping his sister up. The dog got up too, ready to follow the kids.

'Sorry boy, you have to stay,' Lilly said giving him a little bit of meat from the day before. As the siblings walked, a pack of wolves jumped in front of them, but these were definitely not friendly.

'Get behind me Lilly,' Gary whispered as one of the wolves walked towards them growling furiously. Just then the husky ran and stood in front of the kids barking loudly. All the while the pack of wolves moved to circle them.

'Gary what's going on?' Lilly gasped shivering behind her brother. Gary grabbed a stick and swung it around his head to scare them. As the wolves backed away in fear, the husky turned to nudge Lilly's fingers.

'Oh, it's you boy,' she gasped jumping as the wet nose rubbed against her hand.

'Lilly come on,' he said. The dog sat there looking at them with a hopeful expression on his face.

'Aww, can we keep him?' Lilly begged. Gary smiled and sighed.

'Fine,' he said. 'I guess he'll follow us anyway.'

They started to walk in what they hoped was the direction of the city.

A couple hours later, the two kids arrived at a farm where cows and sheep were grazing, in great paddocks full of fresh grass and hay. Suddenly a dog's bark echoed through the forest. The siblings were just about to turn around to run, when a big golden Labrador with reddish tinges to his fur sat down in front of them wagging his tail so fast Gary and Lilly thought it might fall off. The two kids were too busy laughing at the dog's funny personality, they hadn't realised a man was walking up behind them.

'I see you two like dogs,' he said kindly kneeling down to stroke the two dogs with them.

'What's his name?' asked Lilly rubbing his round tummy.

'Uluru, because of his reddish fur,' the man said.

Gary and Lilly stroked the dog for another minute before getting up to go. They didn't want to hang around for too long in case he was friendly with the bad men like the baker and his wife were.

'Bye,' the kids chorused. They walked towards the fields, hoping it was the shortest way home. As the sun started going down, they found an old outbuilding with a tap so they could get a drink.

'Do you want to keep on going?' Gary asked, sitting down next to Lilly. He looked at her and realised she was fast asleep, 'Good night sis,' he whispered leaning on her shoulder. Soon he was sleeping too.

CHAPTER 12: The trap.

Gary sat up the next morning and woke Lilly up so they could keep going home. Lilly sat up rubbing her eyes.

'You're awake, good let's go,' he said. Lilly pulled her hair back.

'Okay I'm up,' she said cupping her hands under the tap to put water in. After a long sip of water, Gary and Lilly stepped forwards and tripped over, they turned around. The man stood there, a mean smirk on his face.

'Sorry kids, nothing personal, I need the cash,' he said gruffly grabbing their arms and pulling them along the grass.

'Ow, what do mean about money, where are you taking us?' Gary asked. The man turned to look at them.

'The person who can find two kids, a boy and a girl, and bring them back to their family gets two thousand bucks. So, I am not letting anyone take my money, so let's go,' he yelled rudely before pulling them along the ground once again.

Alarm bells went in Gary's head as he knew his parents didn't have that sort of money. It must be the bad guys trying to get them back.

Gary looked around and came up with a plan. Lilly looked at him. Gary pursed his lips and started whistling. As he whistled, the husky leaped over a fence, teeth bared as his fangs went into the man's arm.

'Ahhh stupid dog,' he yelled trying to push him off. As he tried to do that Gary and Lilly ran away as fast as they could. The dog ran after them barking his head off, as they all ran back into the forest.

'I hope he didn't see us come this way,' Lilly said trying to catch her breath. She turned around to see Gary behind her.

'I don't think he did, but we better keep running just in case,' he said, the dog sat down next to them as they caught their breath.

'We need a name for him,' Lilly said stroking his ears. 'He's coming with us.'

'Come on Lilly, we can worry about that later,' Gary said. 'For now, we need to get out of here.' He stood up and started running again.

'Gary, wait up,' Lilly hissed. She jumped up and she and the dog bolted after him. The two kids ran until they couldn't hear the man's angry shouts.

'Don't do that again,' Lilly said trying to catch her breath when they felt safe enough to stop.

'Okay, I won't,' Gary said wiping down a rock before she sat.

As the two of them rested, a cheerful voice echoed through the forest followed by a series of other voices and dogs barking. Gary and Lilly crept towards them not knowing what to expect.

They hid in some bushes and watched as people wandered by them. The two kids looked to see where the people were walking to and realised there was a small village with a market in the town square. The two kids carefully stepped out of the bushes as soon as they heard the words 'fresh bread,' hoping they could find something to eat.

CHAPTER 13: A small village.

The siblings stepped into the market, looking around to see what was there. They felt safe in the crowd of people, especially as they couldn't see any men in blue boiler suits.

'Hey, Gary, over here,' Lilly called from outside a toy shop. Gary ran up to the shop and saw the dog, its head inside a bucket of toys

'Sher burra bombui,' the woman yelled crossly. Gary realised the woman was angry, so he pulled Lilly and the dog away, from her shop before she called the town's police.

'Lilly, this way,' he said. He grabbed the dog's puppy skin as they went by another shop, looking for something to eat.

'This is pretty,' Lilly said picking up a necklace with a dragon pendant on it.

'Lilly, we don't have money, and we came here to eat, not buy jewellery,' Gary said grabbing her wrist before she could pick up another necklace.

'There's the food carts,' she said pulling away from Gary's holds, the dog ran after her.

'Lilly!!' Gary shouted, 'what the hell?' he added under his breath as he ran after her and deeper into the massive crowd.

'There you are,' he said crossly when he found them in front of a sandwich cart in the far corner.

'Don't be cross Gary,' Lilly said turning around to look at him the dog woofed sadly to agree with her.

'Okay,' he said more gently this time, he patted the dog's head. 'Come on Lilly, let's go get some food,' he said.

As Gary tried to snatch some bread, Lilly sat down under the nearest tree. The dog curled up on her lap as her brother ran towards them with two loaves of bread in his hands.

'Okay, I think I might be done here,' he said before helping his sister up. 'We need to get out of here before anyone notices missing bread.'

'I think so too,' Lilly gasped pointing at the other end of the square. Gary turned to see what was happening and sure enough, two men in distinctive blue boilersuits were terrorising a young woman.

'Come on Lilly, let's go,' Gary said quickly walking towards the exit of the town, away from the bad guys, his sister and the dog close behind him. The siblings walked out of the town, trying not to draw attention to themselves.

They kept walking until they couldn't hear the village anymore and were certain the bad guys hadn't seen them. They stopped for a rest.

'Wow it's like it's been forever since I heard silence,' Lilly said softly. Gary nodded and rolled his eyes, thinking it hadn't even been a day that they were in the village. He then motioned for Lilly to keep walking. The siblings walked until they arrived at a fast-moving river.

Lilly stepped forwards but slipped, going headfirst into the water. Strong currents pushed Lilly underwater. Gary tried to grab her when her head came up. He grabbed her hand and pulled her out.

'Uhhhh!' he yelled as she got on the bank of the river. The dog ran towards them, barking.

'Wow, that river is strong,' she said, panting heavily.

'Yeah, it is,' he said helping his sister sit up, the dog sat on her other side.

Once Lilly recovered, they walked on, only stopping a couple times to rest as Lilly was still tired.

'Oof!' Lilly cried as she slipped on the ground beneath them, Gary caught her arm as she went towards a tree.

'No more injures for you,' he said holding her hand tightly so she wouldn't go anywhere.

'Gary let go,' Lilly said trying to pull away.

Just then the bad men from the village jumped out in front of them.

'You're coming with us,' one said.

CHAPTER 14: Uncle Bob.

Gary and Lilly stared in shock at the sight of the men.

'Umm, Gary what now??' Lilly asked quietly her eyes full of terror as one of the men tried to grab her. The other man was aiming a crossbow at them when a voice echoed through the forest.

'Hey! Back off! Get lost! Shoo!!' the voice said. Just then a man ran through the forest towards them. The men mumbled but then quickly ran away when they realized the man was armed.

Gary stood in front of his sister, his hands shaking as the guy walked towards him.

'Stay away I am armed,' Gary said his voice shaking as he leaned down to grab a stick, but Lilly stopped him.

'Uncle Bob?' she squeaked. The guy smiled and put down his gun as the two kids ran towards him. He leaned down and hugged them.

'We are so happy to see you,' Gary said staring at their uncle in disbelief.

'You know staring is rude right??' Uncle Bob laughed ruffling the kid's hair. 'But I'm so happy to see you both too. We've all been looking for you.'

'Ow!!' Lilly exclaimed as Uncle Bob's fingers got caught in her messy hair.

'Who is this cutie?' Uncle Bob asked, reaching down to pat the dog.

'He helped us get this far,' Lilly said. 'He doesn't have a name yet.'

Uncle Bob patted the dog a bit longer, then stood up.

'Come on, guys, let's get you home,' Uncle Bob said, leading them through the forest to where his jeep was parked, not far away.

They followed their uncle to his jeep and the dog wandered close behind them.

'No buddy you stay here, this is your home, and you belong here,' Gary said his vision was blurry as he held back tears, the dog whimpered and jumped up to lick his face. But I want to come with you his eyes seemed to say. Gary shook his head sadly and Lilly patted the dog's head before climbing into the car.

'It's OK, you can bring the dog with you,' Uncle Bob said and called the dog. The dog jumped into the car and put his paw on Gary's knee. The kids ruffled the dog's hair.

'Hey boy, you are coming too!' Lilly laughed, the dog wagged his tail and barked. Lilly giggled as Gary pushed the dog into the middle seat.

'So, I guess we're going to have two dogs when we get home,' he said as he put his seatbelt on then he helped Lilly put hers on.

Uncle Bob started up the car.

'It's getting late, we'll stop at my place for the night and head to your house first thing in the morning,' Uncle Bob said. 'I can get a message to your parents, so they know you're safe.'

Gary and Lilly didn't hear him as they were both curled up, fast asleep in the back seat with their dog.

The jeep drove down the road zooming through puddles. It wasn't long before they drove up a long driveway and arrived outside a massive mansion.

'Kids, wake up, we're here,' Uncle Bob said when the car stopped.

The kids yawned and stretched.

'Where are we?' Lilly asked, peering through the darkness that had settled as they were driving.

'We're at my place,' Uncle Bob said. 'I'll get you home in the morning.'

Uncle Bob climbed out of the car and walked up the fancy walkway to the front door. A man opened it and bowed to their uncle before closing as they both went inside. Seconds later a lady rushed out of a side room, followed by a black dog and four puppies. She greeted them in the hallway.

'I can't believe you're here,' she said pulling them into a hug. 'I'm so glad you're alright!'

'Aunt Maggie,' Lilly complained, 'I can't breathe!' Aunt Maggie laughed and let her go. The dog bounded into the house and greeted the black dog and her puppies. It was noisy chaos.

'Maisie, calm down you silly girl,' said Aunt Maggie. She picked up one of the puppies and led the dog and the puppies back to the side room. Gary and Lilly's dog tried to follow. Gary grabbed him gently around the neck to stop him going with them.

'And who is this,' Aunt Maggie asked stroking the dog's ears when everything had calmed down.

'That's our friend he doesn't have a name yet,' Lilly explained leaning down to rub the dog's belly.

'What about Hope?' Their aunt suggested as she sat down in a nearby chair.

'You know what, I love it,' Gary said patting the dog on the head.

'Hi, Hope, are you a Hope?' Lilly asked, and Hope barked to agree wagging his tail so fast it was just a big blur.

'I'd take that as a yes,' Gary laughed as Hope licked them all over the face. Aunt Maggie let the other dogs out for a play and both kids played with them all for a little bit longer before they started to yawn.

'Oh no,' said Aunt Maggie, 'You must both be so tired and hungry. Come through to the kitchen for some food, then I'll show you to the guest bedroom where you can have a bath and sleep.'

They followed their aunt to the kitchen where she prepared toasted cheese sandwiches. They ate hungrily and nearly fell asleep before finishing their food. Aunt Maggie smiled.

'I think we should forget the bath and put you both to bed,' she said. Gary and Lilly agreed. They followed her to the guest bedroom and were asleep before their heads hit the pillow with Hope, Maisie, and her puppies curling up at their feet.

CHAPTER 15: The Next Morning

Lilly groaned in annoyance as her brother pulled the sheet off the bed to wake her up.

'Go away,' Lilly said and tried to get the sheet back on.

Before Gary could say anything, Hope jumped up on the bed and licked Lilly's face. Aunt Maggie came into the room.

'Come on, lazy bug, it's already 12 o'clock,' she said, teasing them. 'Just kidding, it's just after 8am, I thought you needed sleep, Gary's already had a bath. Let's get you cleaned up, fed, then we'll hit the road to get you home.'

Lilly was wide awake then and jumped out of bed.

'I'm starving, can I have food first?' she said.

'I second that,' said Gary, 'I'm hungry too.'

Hope barked in agreement. Aunt Maggie laughed at the three of them.

'Come on, then,' she said. 'Food is ready downstairs.'

Lilly and Gary followed Aunt Maggie and were amazed at the spread of food that greeted them. There were croissants, fresh fruit, a variety of cereals, and more.

'Eat up, kids,' said Uncle Bob, meeting them in the dining room. 'If there's something else you'd like, just let us know.'

'This is awesome,' whispered Lilly to Gary. Gary had his mouth full and just nodded.

It didn't take them long to be full of food. Lilly went up to have a bath and put on some fresh clothes, and they got in the car with Uncle Bob and Hope.

As they pulled out of the drive, they turned to wave to Aunt Maggie, Maisie and the puppies. Uncle Bob turned on the radio in time for the news.

'Reports have been coming from the local jungle about sightings of a man dragging a child away from a local village. Further details in the bulletin in half an hour.'

'Do you think they could be the men who kidnapped us?' Lilly asked.

Gary shrugged.

'Maybe,' he said. 'If they are the same men, maybe they'll get caught and all the kids can go home.'

After hearing the headlines, Uncle Bob changed the station to one that played music only, so they didn't get any further updates on what was happening.

Gary stared out of the window and watched the trees rush past him. He wished he hadn't eaten quite so much as now he was feeling a bit sick.

Hope moved her head onto Gary's knee. Stroking it helped him feel a bit better.

'I hope Mum and Dad will let us keep Hope,' Gary said.

'I'm sure they will,' Lilly replied. 'I'm sure Coco will love Hope and they'll be best friends.'

Gary smiled.

'I hope Mum and Dad took good care of Coco while we were away.'

The siblings were quiet and watched the scenery change from jungle to open fields.

As the sun was starting to set, they reached the outskirts of the city, and they realized they were getting closer to home.

Unfamiliar streets and buildings soon gave way to more familiar ones.

'Shouldn't be too much longer now, kids,' said Uncle Bob. Gary and Lilly started to feel excited. After everything they had been through, they were nearly home. Even Hope started to yip in excitement, picking up on their mood.

'I can't wait to get home,' said Lilly.

'Me too,' said Gary.

Just then, Uncle Bob's car turned into their
street, and they could see their house.

CHAPTER 16: Home safe and sound

Uncle Bob stopped the car in front of their house and Gary, Lilly, and Hope climbed out of the car as quickly as they could, without falling over, and ran to the front door.

Before they could knock, the door was flung open, and they were held in the most massive bear hugs by their parents and grandma. Hope and Coco were both barking and running around their legs in excitement.

'You're home!' exclaimed Mum when they finally let go. 'Are you okay?'

'Barely,' Lilly said. Gary jabbed her in the side. 'Ow!'

'We are okay now,' Gary said. 'We're so happy to be home.'

'Come and have some food,' said Gran. They all moved to the kitchen and let Gran feed them.

'Who is this?' asked Dad, patting Hope's head after they were all sitting at the table.

'That's Hope,' said Lilly. 'She helped us make it home, can we keep her?'

'Anyone who helps my kids is welcome here,' replied Dad. 'Of course she can stay.'

'Hooray!' said Lilly, giving Hope a hug. Coco jumped up for some attention too. 'Don't worry, Coco, I didn't forget you.' Lilly picked Coco up and placed him on her lap for hugs.

'We should let the authorities know the kids are back,' Gran said. They all agreed, Dad and Uncle Bob went to notify the police while

Lilly and Gary played with the dogs, happier than they could describe to be home.

CHAPTER 17: Six months later

'REWARD FOR CHILDREN HAILED HEROES' the headline in the local paper read. It had been six months since Gary and Lilly had been kidnapped and the information they provided, along with the eyewitness sightings helped the authorities find the bad guys, their camp, and free all the children.

The reward money was enough for Gary and Lilly's family to move out of the city to a small farm where Lilly could have her own horse and Gary was able to learn archery.

Hope and Coco became the best of friends, most of the time, and they loved the space on the farm.

The farm was closer to Uncle Bob and Aunt Maggie, so they were able to spend more time together.

After school one day, Gary and Lilly stopped by the letterbox, it was stuffed full of letters for them from the kids they had helped rescue.

One letter stood out:

Dear Gary,

Thank you for escaping and letting the authorities know what you had seen so they could find us.

I am now back home and at school. I never want to sweep anything ever again!

I hope we can meet up again one day.

From your friend, Justin.

'Who's Justin?' Lilly asked.

'I met him on my first day at the camp,' said Gary. 'He was also the kid in the photo at the bakery, the one with six fingers that looked strange. I'm glad he's safely back home again.'

'It's good that all the kids are home safely,' said Lilly, looking at a letter of her own.

They looked up and saw their mum and dad walking to the house from the fields.

'I'm glad everything has worked out for all of us,' said Lilly.

'Me too,' said Gary.

The siblings got up to meet their parents followed by Hope and Coco.

About the Author

Baylee Carlyon is a proud Yorta Yorta girl, who was born in Benalla. She is currently living between Phillip Island and St Kilda in Victoria and is attending Sophia Mundi Steiner  School in Abbotsford. She is lucky to live between both places, getting the most out of both city and coastal living, spending every Friday to Sunday and holidays on the island.

Baylee loves reading, writing, cooking, drawing, singing and song writing. She loves spending time with her large extended family and learning from people within her community. Recently, Baylee has entered artwork in two NAIDOC exhibitions.

Her artwork shows her love for nature,
especially her love for birds and other animals.
She only started drawing as a hobby about a
year and a half ago. Her work shows how
creative and talented she is.

Acknowledgements

Melissa - I would like to thank my mentor, Melissa, for helping me with finishing my book and supporting me throughout this incredible journey. I could never thank you enough for everything you've done for me.

Barry - I would like to thank my dad Barry for supporting me over a long distance throughout this adventure and never giving up on me. I would also like to thank him for his jokes and for cheering me up when things got stressful.

Louise - I would like to thank my mum for supporting me in my project and throughout my life. Thanks to her, I was able to get my book finished and published, I never would have found Melissa without her.

Thanks Mum

Stella - I would like to thank my teacher, Stella, for everything she has done for me including teaching and supporting me throughout Year 8 and the Year 8 project. I will never be able to thank you enough for everything you've done for me.

Audrey - I would like to thank my dog, Audrey, for mostly being by my side and sometimes not bugging me, which is never.

My cousins - For encouraging and supporting me, especially the boys who were enthusiastic and gave me inspiration.